Geraldine Durrant

Pirate Gran

illustrated by Rose Forshall

NATIONAL
MARITIME
MUSEUM

Gran's **great.** She bakes and knits, and
says things like "take your coat off indoors
or you won't feel the benefit."

You'd never guess
she'd been a **pirate**
when she was younger.

Back then she sailed aboard the **Black Barnacle**
with her shipmates Flint-Hearted Jack,
Fingers O'Malley and Cut-Throat Malone –

She had red hair and striped stockings
and drank sherry. Pirates mostly drink rum,
but Gran says sherry is more ladylike.

Pirating isn't the life for everyone, but Gran says
if you don't mind sleeping in a hammock and being
called Scary Mary or Mad Moll, then it's a career
more girls should think about.

Long hours of course, but you get to travel — and if you like eating fish and bird-watching it's ideal really.

Gran doesn't do pirating any more. But she still wears her old pirate hat round the house,

and carves the roast with her cutlass. She says it reminds her of "the good times".

And she keeps a **crocodile** under her bed.

He's pretty harmless really, although if he's in a bad mood she has to run from the bedroom door and leap on to her mattress so he doesn't nip her ankles.

But Gran's pretty spry for her age.
Her reverse three-and-a-half-somersaults
tuck is amazing, but Gran's very modest.

She says it's "just some old thing"
she picked up from Gentleman Jim Jones,
"that time he walked the plank."

It was Jim who gave her the crocodile and
Grandpa says she spoils it. She always
cooks up a nice bit of fish for its supper . . .

. . . and on its birthday she bakes her
special crocodile Dundee cake.
It is a bit sea-weedy for some, but it makes
a change from chocolate sponge.

And her Chicken Surprise is **brilliant.**
The surprise is it's made with whelks, but Gran
says when you are at sea you've got to make do.

Grandpa found out the hard way that her ice-cream bombe is made with real gunpowder...

...but Gran said he only had himself to blame for smoking at the dinner table.

BANG!

And she was a real sport
about rescuing him.

It's not the first time she's
fished Grandpa out of trouble.

When they met, her shipmates had hung him up by his heels and were shaking coins out of his pockets.

Gran was furious.

"Unhand that landlubber or I'll keelhaul every man jack of you," she said.

And trust me, when Gran's mad . . .

...you **don't** want to upset her.

"Love at first fright," was what Grandpa called it, so with Gran the prettiest pirate ever to sail the seven seas, he asked the Captain to marry them at once.

Gran's veil was ten metres of fine fish-net, and she carried a coral bouquet . . .

. . . and afterwards everyone danced hornpipes on the poop deck till dawn, when they waved Gran goodbye.

Gran bought a little cottage with her pirate gold
and settled down by the seaside with Grandpa.

But even though she has Grandpa and the crocodile for company I know she sometimes misses her old shipmates Flint-Hearted Jack, Fingers O'Malley and Cut-Throat Malone.

So she tucks us into our hammocks and tells us tales of her pirate past.

Then she and the crocodile take out their teeth and snuggle under the eiderdown . . .

. . . snoring quietly as
they dream about the
bad old days aboard the
Black Barnacle.

For Patrick and my little shipmates, Eleanor and Alice.

This book was developed from the winning entry to the
BBC London / RaW 60 second story-writing competition. RaW is the
BBC's biggest ever campaign to help adults across the UK to build
their confidence in reading and writing, by telling stories to their children.

A CIP catalogue record for this book is available from the British Library.

First published in the UK in 2008 by the National Maritime Museum, Greenwich, London SE10 9NF

www.nmm.ac.uk/publishing

Text © Geraldine Durrant, 2008 and illustrations © Rose Forshall, 2008

Hardback: 978-0-948065-96-5   Paperback: 978-1-906367-07-7

Printed in China